MARK · TWAIN

THE
STOLEN WHITE
ELEPHANT

MARK · TWAIN

THE STOLEN WHITE ELEPHANT

Illustrated by Robert Ingpen

National Library of Australia
Cataloguing-in-Publication data

Twain, Mark, 1835-1910.
   The stolen white elephant.

   ISBN 0 9587845 2 3

   1. Elephants — Juvenile fiction. I. Ingpen, Robert,
   1936-   . II. Title.

813'.4

Illustrations © 1987 by Robert Ingpen

Produced by P.I.C. Pty Ltd
Box 4939, GPO Sydney, Australia 2001

First published in Australia by Ashton Scholastic Pty Limited 1987.

Printed in Hong Kong

PROLOGUE

Left out of *A Tramp Abroad*, because it was feared that some of the particulars had been exaggerated, and that others were not true. Before these suspicions had been proven groundless, the book had gone to press. M.T.

I

The following curious history was related to me by a chance railway acquaintance. He was a gentleman more than seventy years of age, and his thoroughly good and gentle face and earnest and sincere manner imprinted the unmistakable stamp of truth upon every statement which fell from his lips. He said:

You know in what reverence the royal white elephant of Siam is held by the people of that country. You know it is sacred to kings, only kings may possess it, and that it is indeed in a measure even superior to kings, since it receives not merely honor but worship. Very well; five years ago, when the troubles concerning the frontier line arose between Great Britain and Siam, it was presently manifest that Siam had been in the wrong. Therefore every reparation was quickly made, and the British representative stated that he was satisfied and the past should be forgotten. This

greatly relieved the King of Siam, and partly as a token of gratitude, but partly also, perhaps, to wipe out any little remaining vestige of unpleasantness which England might feel toward him, he wished to send the Queen a present—the sole sure way of propitiating an enemy, according to Oriental ideas. This present ought not only to be a royal one, but transcendently royal. Wherefore, what offering could be so meet as that of a white elephant? My position in the Indian civil service was such that I was deemed peculiarly worthy of the honor of conveying the present to Her Majesty. A ship was fitted out for me and my servants and the officers and attendants of the elephant, and in due time I arrived in New York harbor and placed my royal charge in admirable quarters in Jersey City. It was necessary to remain awhile in order to recruit the animal's health before resuming the voyage.

All went well during a fortnight—then my calamities began. The white elephant was stolen! I was called up at dead of night and informed of this fearful misfortune. For some moments I was beside myself with terror and anxiety; I was helpless. Then I grew calmer and collected my faculties. I soon saw my course—for indeed there was but the one course for an intelligent man to pursue. Late as it was, I flew to New York and got a policeman to conduct me to the headquarters of the detective force. Fortunately I arrived in time, though the chief of the force, the celebrated Inspector Blunt, was just on the point of leaving for his home. He was a man of middle size and compact frame, and when he was thinking deeply he had a way of knitting his brows and tapping his forehead reflectively with his finger, which impressed you at once with the conviction that you stood in

the presence of a person of no common order. The very sight of him gave me confidence and made me hopeful. I stated my errand. It did not flurry him in the least; it had no more visible effect upon his iron self-possession than if I had told him somebody had stolen my dog. He motioned me to a seat, and said calmly—

'Allow me to think a moment, please.'

So saying, he sat down at his coffee table and leaned his head upon his hand. Several clerks were at work at the other end of the room; the scratching of their pens was all the sound I heard during the next six or seven minutes. Meantime the inspector sat there buried in thought. Finally he raised his head, and there was that in the firm lines of his face which showed me that his brain had done its work and his plan was made. Said he—and his voice was low and impressive:

'This is no ordinary case. Every step must be warily taken; each step must be made sure before the next is ventured. And secrecy must be observed—secrecy profound and absolute. Speak to no one about the matter, not even the reporters. I will take care of *them*; I will see that they get only what it may suit my ends to let them know.' He touched a bell; a youth appeared. 'Alaric, tell the reporters to remain for the present.' The boy retired. 'Now let us proceed to business—and systematically. Nothing can be accomplished in this trade of mine without strict and minute method.'

He took a pen and some paper. 'Now—name of the elephant?'

'Hassan Ben Ali Ben Selim Abdallah Mohammed Moise Alhammal Jamsetjejeebbey Dhuleep Sultan Ebu Bhudpoor.'

'Very well. Given name?'

9

'Jumbo.'

'Very well. Place of birth?'

'The capital city of Siam.'

'Parents living?'

'No—dead.'

'Had they any other issue besides this one?'

'None—he was an only child.'

'Very well. These matters are sufficient under that head. Now please describe the elephant, and leave out no particular, however insignificant—that is, insignificant from *your* point of view. To men in my profession there *are* no insignificant particulars; they do not exist.'

I described; he wrote. When I was done, he said:

'Now listen. If I have made any mistakes, correct me.'

He read as follows:

'Height, 19 feet; length, from apex of forehead to insertion of tail, 26 feet; length of trunk, 16 feet; length of tail, 6 feet; total length, including trunk and tail, 48 feet; length of tusks, 9½ feet; ears in keeping with these dimensions; footprint resembles the mark when one up-ends a barrel in the snow; color of the elephant, a dull white; has a hole the size of a plate in each ear for the insertion of jewelry, and possesses the habit in a remarkable degree of squirting water upon spectators and of maltreating with his trunk not only such persons as he is acquainted with, but even entire strangers; limps slightly with his right hind leg, and has a small scar in his left armpit caused by a former boil; had on, when stolen, a castle containing seats for fifteen persons, and a gold-cloth saddle-blanket the size of an ordinary carpet.'

There were no mistakes. The inspector touched the bell, handed the description to Alaric, and said:

'Have fifty thousand copies of this printed at once and mailed to every detective office and pawnbroker's shop on the continent.' Alaric retired. 'There—so far, so good. Next, I must have a photograph of the property.'

I gave him one. He examined it critically, and said:

'It must do, since we can do no better; but he has his trunk curled up and tucked into his mouth. That is unfortunate, and is calculated to mislead, for of course he does not usually have it in that position.' He touched his bell.

'Alaric, have fifty thousand copies of this photograph made, the first thing in the morning, and mail them with the descriptive circulars.'

Alaric retired to execute his orders. The inspector said:

'It will be necessary to offer a reward, of course. Now as to the amount?'

'What sum would you suggest?'

'To *begin* with, I should say—well, twenty-five thousand dollars. It is an intricate and difficult business; there are a thousand avenues of escape and opportunities of conceal-ment. These thieves have friends and pals everywhere—'

'Bless me, do you know who they are?'

The wary face, practised in concealing the thoughts and feelings within, gave me no token, nor yet the replying words, so quietly uttered:

'Never mind about that. I may, and I may not. We generally gather a pretty shrewd inkling of who our man is by the manner of his work and the size of the game he goes after. We are not dealing with a pickpocket or a hall thief, now, make up your mind to that. This property was not "lifted" by

12

a novice. But, as I was saying, considering the amount of travel which will have to be done, and the diligence with which the thieves will cover up their traces as they move along, twenty-five thousand may be too small a sum to offer, yet I think it worth while to start with that.'

So we determined upon that figure, as a beginning. Then this man, whom nothing escaped which could by any possibility be made to serve as a clue, said:

'There are cases in detective history to show that criminals have been detected through peculiarities in their appetites. Now, what does this elephant eat, and how much?'

'Well, as to *what* he eats—he will eat *anything*. He will eat a man, he will eat a Bible—he will eat anything *between* a man and a Bible.'

'Good—very good indeed, but too general. Details are necessary—details are the only valuable things in our trade. Very well—as to men. At one meal—or, if you prefer, during one day—how many men will he eat, if fresh?'

'He would not care whether they are fresh or not; at a single meal he would eat five ordinary men.'

'Very good; five men; we will put that down. What nationalities would he prefer?'

'He is indifferent about nationalities. He prefers acquaintances, but is not prejudiced against strangers.'

'Very good. Now as to Bibles. How many Bibles would he eat at a meal?'

'He would eat an entire edition.'

'It is hardly succinct enough. Do you mean the ordinary octavo, or the family illustrated?'

'I think he would be indifferent to illustrations; I think he would not value illustrations above simple letterpress.'

'No, you do not get my idea. I refer to bulk. The ordinary octavo Bible weighs about two pounds and a half while the great quarto with the illustrations weighs ten or twelve. How many Doré Bibles would he eat at a meal?'

'If you know this elephant, you could not ask. He would take what they had.'

'Well, put it in dollars and cents, then. We must get at it somehow. The Doré costs a hundred dollars a copy, Russian leather, bevelled.'

'He would require about fifty thousand dollars' worth—say an edition of five hundred copies.'

'Now, that is more exact. I will put that down. Very well; he likes men and Bibles; so far, so good. What else will he eat? I want particulars.'

'He will leave Bibles to eat bricks, he will leave bricks to eat bottles, he will leave bottles to eat clothing, he will leave clothing to eat cats, he will leave cats to eat oysters, he will leave oysters to eat ham, he will leave ham to eat sugar, he will leave sugar to eat pie, he will leave pie to eat potatoes, he will leave potatoes to eat bran, he will leave bran to eat hay, he will leave hay to eat oats, he will leave oats to eat rice for he was mainly raised on it. There is nothing whatever that he will not eat but European butter, and he would eat that if he could taste it.'

'Very good. General quantity at a meal—say about——'

'Well, anywhere from a quarter to half a ton.'

'And he drinks——'

'Everything that is fluid. Milk, water, whisky, molasses, castor oil, camphene, carbolic acid—it is no use to go into particulars; whatever fluid occurs to you set it down. He will drink anything that is fluid, except European coffee.'

14

'Very good. As to quantity?'

'Put it down five to fifteen barrels—his thirst varies; his other appetites do not.'

'These things are unusual. They ought to furnish quite good clues toward tracing him.'

He touched the bell.

'Alaric, summon Captain Burns.'

Burns appeared. Inspector Blunt unfolded the whole matter to him, detail by detail. Then he said in the clear, decisive tones of a man whose plans are clearly defined in his head, and who is accustomed to command:

'Captain Burns, detail Detectives Jones, Davis, Halsey, Bates, and Hackett to shadow the elephant.'

'Yes, sir.'

'Detail Detectives Moses, Dakin, Murphy, Rogers, Tupper, Higgins, and Bartholomew to shadow the thieves.'

'Yes, sir.'

'Place a strong guard—a guard of thirty picked men, with a relief of thirty—over the place from whence the elephant was stolen, to keep strict watch there night and day, and allow none to approach—except reporters—without written authority from me.'

'Yes, sir.'

'Place detectives in plain clothes in the railway, steamship, and ferry depôts, and upon all roadways leading out of Jersey City, with orders to search all suspicious persons.'

'Yes, sir.'

'Furnish all these men with photograph and accompanying descriptions of the elephant, and instruct them to search all trains and outgoing ferry-boats and other vessels.'

'Yes, sir.'

16

'If the elephant should be found, let him be seized, and the information forwarded to me by telegraph.'

'Yes, sir.'

'Let me be informed at once if any clues should be found—footprints of the animal, or anything of that kind.'

'Yes, sir.'

'Get an order commanding the harbor police to patrol the frontages vigilantly.'

'Yes, sir.'

'Despatch detectives in plain clothes over all the railways, north as far as Canada, west as far as Ohio, south as far as Washington.'

'Yes, sir.'

'Place experts in all the telegraph offices to listen to all messages; and let them require that all cipher despatches be interpreted to them.'

'Yes, sir.'

'Let all these things be done with the utmost secrecy—mind, the most impenetrable secrecy.'

'Yes, sir.'

'Report to me promptly at the usual hour.'

'Yes, sir.'

'Go!'

'Yes, sir.'

He was gone.

Inspector Blunt was silent and thoughtful a moment, while the fire in his eye cooled down and faded out. Then he turned to me and said in a placid voice:

'I am not given to boasting, it is not my habit; but—we shall find the elephant.'

I shook him warmly by the hand and thanked him; and I *felt* my thanks, too. The more I had seen of the man the more I liked him, and the more I admired and marvelled over the mysterious wonders of his profession. Then we parted for the night, and I went home with a far happier heart than I had carried with me to his office.

II

Next morning it was all in the newspapers, in the minutest detail. It even had additions—consisting of Detective This, Detective That, and Detective The Other's 'Theory' as to how the robbery was done, who the robbers were, and whither they had flown with their booty. There were eleven of these theories, and they covered all the possibilities; and this single fact shows what independent thinkers detectives are. No two theories were alike, or even much resembled each other, save in one striking particular, and in that one

all the eleven theories were absolutely agreed. That was, that although the rear of my building was torn out and the only door remained locked, the elephant had not been removed through the rent, but by some other (undiscovered) outlet. All agreed that the robbers had made that rent only to mislead the detectives. That never would have occured to me or to any other layman, perhaps, but it had not deceived the detectives for a moment. Thus, what I had supposed was the only thing that had no mystery about it was in fact the very thing I had gone furthest astray in. The eleven theories all named the supposed robbers, but no two named the same robbers; the total number of suspected persons was thirty-seven. The various newspaper accounts all closed with the most important opinion of all—that of Chief Inspector Blunt. A portion of this statement read as follows:

'The chief knows who the two principals are, namely, "Brick" Duffy and "Red" McFadden. Ten days before the robbery was achieved he was already aware that it was to be attempted, and had quietly proceeded to shadow these two noted villains; but unfortunately on the night in question their track was lost, and before it could be found again the bird was flown—that is, the elephant.

'Duffy and McFadden are the boldest scoundrels in the profession; the chief has reason for believing that they are the men who stole the stove out of the detective headquarters on a bitter night last winter—in consequence of which the chief and every detective were in the hands of the physicians before morning, some with frozen feet, others with frozen fingers, ears, and other members.'

When I read the first half of that I was more astonished than ever at the wonderful sagacity of this strange man. He

not only saw everything in the present with a clear eye, but even the future could not be hidden from him. I was soon at his office, and said I could not help wishing he had had those men arrested, and so prevented the trouble and loss; but his reply was simple and unanswerable:

'It is not our province to prevent crime, but to punish it. We cannot punish it until it is committed.'

I remarked that the secrecy with which we had begun had been marred by the newspapers; not only all our facts but all our plans and purposes had been revealed; even all the suspected persons had been named; these would doubtless disguise themselves now, or go into hiding.

'Let them. They will find that when I am ready for them, my hand will descend upon them, in their secret places, as unerringly as the hand of fate. As to the newspapers, we *must* keep in with them. Fame, reputation, constant public mention—these are the detective's bread and butter. He must publish his facts, else he will be supposed to have none; he must publish his theory, for nothing is so strange or striking as a detective's theory, or brings him so much wondering respect; we must publish our plans, for these the journals insist upon having them, and we could not deny them without offending. We must constantly show the public what we are doing, or they will believe we are doing nothing. It is much pleasanter to have a newspaper say, "Inspector Blunt's ingenious and extraordinary theory is as follows," than to have it say some harsh thing, or, worse still, some sarcastic one.'

'I see the force of what you say. But I noticed that in one part of your remarks in the papers this morning, you refused to reveal your opinion upon a certain minor point.'

'Yes, we always do that; it has a good effect. Besides, I had not formed any opinion on that point, any way.'

I deposited a considerable sum of money with the inspector, to meet current expenses, and sat down to wait for news. We were expecting the telegrams to begin to arrive at any moment now. Meantime I re-read the newspapers and also our descriptive circular, and observed that our $25,000 reward seemed to be offered only to detectives. I said I thought it ought to be offered to anybody who would catch the elephant. The inspector said:

'It is the detectives who will find the elephant, hence the reward will go to the right place. If other people found the animal, it would only be by watching the detectives and taking advantage of clues and indications stolen from them, and that would entitle the detectives to the reward, after all. The proper office of a reward is to stimulate the men who deliver up their time and their trained sagacities to this sort of work, and not to confer benefits upon chance citizens who stumble upon a capture without having earned the benefits by their own merits and labors.'

This was reasonable enough, certainly. Now the telegraphic machine in the corner began to click, and the following despatch was the result:

'Flower Station, N.Y.: 7.30 a.m.

'Have got a clue. Found a succession of deep tracks across a farm near here. Followed them two miles east without result; think elephant went west. Shall now shadow him in that direction.

Darley, *Detective*'

'Darley's one of the best men on the force,' said the inspector. 'We shall hear from him again before long.'

Telegram No. 2 came:

'Barker's, N.J.: 7.40 a.m.

'Just arrived. Glass factory broken open here during night and eight hundred bottles taken. Only water in large quantity near here is five miles distant. Shall strike for there. Elephant will be thirsty. Bottles were empty.

Baker, *Detective*'

'That promises well, too,' said the inspector. 'I told you the creature's appetites would not be bad clues.'

Telegram No. 3:

'Taylorville, L.I.: 8.15 a.m.

'A haystack near here disappeared during night. Probably eaten. Have got a clue, and am off.

Hubbard, *Detective*'

'How he does move around!' said the inspector. 'I knew we had a difficult job on hand, but we shall catch him yet.'

'Flower Station, N.Y.: 9 a.m.

'Shadowed the tracks three miles westward. Large, deep, and ragged. Have just met a farmer who says they are not elephant tracks. Says they are holes where he dug up saplings for shade-trees when ground was frozen last winter. Give me orders how to proceed.

Darley, *Detective*'

'Aha! a confederate of the thieves! The thing grows warm,' said the inspector.

He dictated the following telegram to Darley:

'Arrest the man and force him to name his pals. Continue to follow the tracks—to the Pacific, if necessary.

Chief Blunt'

Next telegram:

'Coney Point, Pa.: 8.45 a.m.

'Gas office broken open here during the night and three months' unpaid gas bills taken. Have got a clue and am away.

Murphy, *Detective*'

'Heavens!' said the inspector, 'would he eat gas bills?'

'Through ignorance—yes; but they cannot support life. At least, unassisted.'

Now came this exciting telegram:

'Just arrived. This village in consternation. Elephant passed through here at five this morning. Some say he went east, some say west, some north, some south—but all say they did not wait to notice particularly. He killed a horse; have secured a piece of it for a clue. Killed it with his trunk; from style of blow, think he struck it left-handed. From position in which horse lies, think elephant travelled north-ward along line of Berkley railway. Has four and a half hours' start; but I move on his track at once.

Hawkes, *Detective*'

I uttered exclamations of joy. The inspector was as self-contained as a graven image. He calmly touched his bell.

'Alaric, send Captain Burns here.'

Burns appeared.

'How many men are ready for instant orders?'

'Ninety-six, sir.'

'Send them north at once. Let them concentrate along the line of the Berkley road north of Ironville.'

'Yes, sir.'

'Let them conduct their movements with the utmost secrecy. As fast as others are at liberty, hold them for orders.'

'Yes, sir.'

'Go!'

'Yes, sir.'

Presently came another telegram:

'Sage Corners, N.Y.: 10.30

'Just arrived. Elephant passed through here at 8.15. All escaped from the town but a policeman. Apparently elephant did not strike at policeman, but at the lamp-post. Got both. I have secured a portion of the policeman as clue.

Stumm, *Detective*'

'So the elephant has turned westward,' said the inspector. 'However, he will not escape, for my men are scattered all over that region.'

The next telegram said:

'Glover's, 11.15.

'Just arrived. Village deserted, except sick and aged. Elephant passed through three-quarters of an hour ago. The anti-temperance mass meeting was in session; he put his trunk in at a window and washed it out with water from cistern. Some swallowed it—since dead; several drowned. Detectives Cross and O'Shaughnessy were passing through town, but going south—so missed elephant. Whole region for many miles around in terror—people flying from their homes. Wherever they turn they meet elephant, and many are killed.

Brant, *Detective*'

I could have shed tears, this havoc so distressed me. But the inspector only said:

'You see—we are closing in on him. He feels our presence; he has turned eastward again.'

Yet further troublous news was in store for us. The telegraph brought this:

'Hoganport, 12.19.

'Just arrived. Elephant passed through half an hour ago, creating wildest fright and excitement. Elephant raged around streets; two plumbers going by, killed one—other escaped. Regret general.

O'Flaherty, *Detective*'

'Now he is right in the midst of my men,' said the inspector. 'Nothing can save him.'

A succession of telegrams came from detectives who were scattered through New Jersey and Pennsylvania, and who were following clues consisting of ravaged barns, factories, and Sunday-school libraries, with high hopes—hopes amounting to certainties, indeed. The inspector said:

'I wish I could communicate with them and order them north, but that is impossible. A detective only visits a telegraph office to send his report; then he is off again, and you don't know where to put your hand on him.'

Now came this despatch:

'Bridgeport, Ct.: 12.15.

'Barnum offers rate of $4,000 a year for exclusive privilege of using elephant as traveling advertising medium from now till detectives find him. Wants to paste circus-posters on him. Desires immediate answer.

Boggs, *Detective*'

'That is perfectly absurd!' I exclaimed.

'Of course it is,' said the inspector. 'Evidently Mr. Barnum, who thinks he is so sharp, does not know me—but I know him.'

Then he dictated this answer to the despatch:

'Mr. Barnum's offer declined. Make it $7,000 or nothing.

Chief Blunt'

'There. We shall not have to wait long for an answer. Mr. Barnum is not at home; he is in the telegraph office—it is his way when he has business on hand. Inside of three—'

34

'Done. — P. T. Barnum.'

So interrupted the clicking telegraphic instrument. Before I could make a comment upon this extraordinary episode, the following despatch carried my thoughts into another and very distressing channel:

'Bolivia, N.Y.: 12.50.

'Elephant arrived here from the south and passed through towards the forest at 11.50, dispersing a funeral on the way, and diminishing the mourners by two. Citizens fired some small cannon-balls into him, and then fled. Detective Burke and I arrived ten minutes later, from the north, but mistook some excavations for footprints, and so lost a good deal of time; but at last we struck the right trail and followed it to the woods. We then got down on our hands and knees and continued to keep a sharp eye on the track, and so shadowed it into the brush. Burke was in advance. Unfortunately the animal had stopped to rest; therefore, Burke having his head down, intent upon the track, butted up against the elephant's hind legs before he was aware of his vicinity. Burke instantly rose to his feet, seized the tail, and exclaimed joyfully, "I claim the re——" but got no further, for a single blow of the huge trunk laid the brave fellow's fragments low in death. I fled rearward, and the elephant turned and shadowed me to the edge of the wood, making tremendous speed, and I should inevitably have been lost, but that the remains of the funeral providentially intervened again and diverted his attention. I have just learned that nothing of that funeral is now left; but this is no loss, for there is an abundance of material for another. Meantime the elephant has disappeared again.

Mulrooney, *Detective*'

35

We heard no news except from the diligent and confident detectives scattered about New Jersey, Pennsylvania, Delaware, and Virginia—who were all following fresh and encouraging clues—until shortly after 2 p.m., when this telegram came:

'Baxter Centre, 2.15.

'Elephant been here, plastered over with circus-bills, and broke up a revival, striking down and damaging many who were on the point of entering upon a better life. Citizens penned him up, and established a guard. When Detective Brown and I arrived, some time after, we entered enclosure and proceeded to identify elephant by photograph and description. All marks tallied exactly except one, which we could not see—the boil-scar under armpit. To make sure, Brown crept under to look, and was immediately brained—that is, head crushed and destroyed, though nothing issued from débris. All fled; so did elephant, striking right and left with much effect. Has escaped, but left bold blood-track from cannon-wounds. Rediscovery certain. He broke southward through a dense forest.

Brent, *Detective*'

That was the last telegram. At nightfall a fog shut down which was so dense that objects but three feet away could not be discerned. This lasted all night. The ferry boats and even the omnibuses had to stop running.

III

Next morning the papers were as full of detective theories as before; they had all our tragic facts in detail also, and a great many more which they had received from their telegraphic correspondents. Column after column was occupied, a third of its way down, with glaring head-lines, which it made my heart sick to read. Their general tone was like this:

'THE WHITE ELEPHANT AT LARGE! HE MOVES UPON HIS FATAL MARCH! WHOLE VILLAGES DESERTED BY THEIR FRIGHT-STRICKEN OCCU-PANTS! PALE TERROR GOES BEFORE HIM, DEATH AND DEVASTATION FOLLOW AFTER! AFTER THESE, THE DETECTIVES. BARNS DESTROYED, FACTORIES GUTTED, HARVESTS DEVOURED, PUBLIC ASSEMBLAGES DISPERSED, ACCOMPANIED BY SCENES OF CARNAGE IMPOSSIBLE TO DESCRIBE! THEORIES OF THIRTY-FOUR OF THE MOST DIS-TINGUISHED DECTECTIVES ON THE FORCE! THEORY OF CHIEF BLUNT!'

'There!' said Inspector Blunt, almost betrayed into excite-ment, 'this is magnificent! This is the greatest windfall that any detective organisation ever had. The fame of it will travel to the ends of the earth, and endure to the end of time, and my name with it.'

But there was no joy for me. I felt as if I had committed all those red crimes, and that the elephant was only my irresponsible agent. And how the list had grown! In one place he had 'interfered with an election and killed five repeaters.' He had followed this act with the destruction of two poor fellows, named O'Donohue and McFlannigan, who had 'found a refuge in the home of the oppressed of all lands only the day before, and were in the act of exercising for the first time the noble right of American citizens at the polls, when stricken down by the relentless hand of the Scourge of Siam.' In another, he had 'found a crazy sensation-preacher preparing his next season's heroic attacks on the dance, the theatre, and other things which can't strike back, and had stepped on him.' And in still another place he had 'killed a lightning-rod agent.' And so the list went on, growing redder and redder, and more and more heart-breaking. Sixty persons had been killed, and two hundred and forty wounded. All the accounts bore just testimony to the activity and devotion of the detectives, and all closed with the remark that 'three hundred thousand citizens and four detectives saw the dread creature, and two of the latter he destroyed.'

I dreaded to hear the telegraphic instrument begin to click again. By-and-by the messages began to pour in, but I was happily disappointed in their nature. It was soon apparent that all trace of the elephant was lost. The fog had enabled him to search out a good hiding-place unobserved. Telegrams from the most absurdly distant points reported that a dim vast mass had been glimpsed there through the fog at such and such an hour, and was 'undoubtedly the elephant.' This dim vast mass had been glimpsed in New Haven, in New Jersey, in Pennsylvania, in interior New York, in Brooklyn,

and even in the city of New York itself! But in all cases the dim vast mass had vanished quickly and left no trace. Every detective of the large force scattered over this huge extent of country sent his hourly report, and each and every one of them had a clue, and was shadowing something, and was hot upon the heels of it.

But the day passed without other result.

The next day the same.

The next just the same.

The newspaper reports began to grow monotonous with facts that amounted to nothing, clues which led to nothing, and theories which had nearly exhausted the elements which surprise and delight and dazzle.

By advice of the inspector I doubled the reward.

Four more dull days followed. Then came a bitter blow to the poor, hard-working detectives—the journalists declined to print their theories, and coldly said, 'Give us a rest.'

Two weeks after the elephant's disappearance I raised the reward to $75,000 by the inspector's advice. It was a great sum, but I felt that I would rather sacrifice my whole private fortune than lose my credit with my Government. Now that the detectives were in adversity, the newspapers turned upon them, and began to fling the most stinging sarcasms at them. This gave the minstrels an idea, and they dressed themselves as detectives and hunted the elephant on the stage in the most extravagant way. The caricaturists made pictures of detectives scanning the country with spy-glasses, while the elephant, at their backs, stole apples out of their pockets. And they made all sorts of ridiculous pictures of the detective badge—you have seen that badge printed in gold on the back of detective novels, no doubt—it is a wide-staring eye, with the legend, 'We Never Sleep.' When detectives called for a drink, the would-be facetious bar-keeper resurrected an obsolete form of expression, and said, 'Will you have an eye-opener?' All the air was thick with sarcasms.

But there was one man who moved calm, untouched, unaffected through it all. It was that heart of oak, the Chief Inspector. His brave eye never drooped, his serene confidence never wavered. He always said:

'Let them rail on; he laughs best who laughs last.'

My admiration for the man grew into a species of worship. I was at his side always. His office had become an unpleasant place to me, and now became daily more and more so. Yet if he could endure it I meant to do so also; at least, as long as I could. So I came regularly, and stayed—the only outsider who seemed to be capable of it. Everybody wondered how I could; and often it seemed to me that I must desert, but at such times I looked into that calm and apparently unconscious face, and held my ground.

About three weeks after the elephant's disappearance I was about to say, one morning, that I should *have* to strike my colors and retire, when the great detective arrested the thought by proposing one more superb and masterly move.

This was to compromise with the robbers. The fertility of this man's invention exceeded anything I have ever seen, and I have had a wide intercourse with the world's finest minds. He said he was confident he could compromise for $100,000 and recover the elephant. I said I believed I could scrape the amount together; but what would become of the poor detectives who had worked so faithfully? He said:

'In compromises they always get half.'

This removed my only objection. So the inspector wrote two notes, in this form:

'Dear Madam, — Your husband can make a large sum of money (and be entirely protected from the law) by making an immediate appointment with me.

Chief Blunt'

He sent one of these by his confidential messenger to the 'reputed wife' of Brick Duffy, and the other to the reputed wife of Red McFadden.

Within the hour these offensive answers came:

'Ye Owld fool: brick McDuffys bin ded 2 yere.

Bridget Mahoney'

'Chief Bat, — Red McFadden is hung and in heving 18 month. Any Ass but a detective knose that.

Mary O'Hooligan'

'I had long suspected these facts,' said the inspector; 'this testimony proves the unerring accuracy of my instinct.'

The moment one resource failed him he was ready with another. He immediately wrote an advertisement for the morning papers, and I kept a copy of it . . .

'A. — xwblv. 242 N. Tjnd — fz328wmlg. Ozpo, — ; 2 m! ogw. Mum.'

He said that if the thief was alive this would bring him to

44

the usual rendezvous. He further explained that the usual rendezvous was a place where all business affairs between detectives and criminals were conducted. This meeting would take place at twelve the next night.

We could do nothing till then, and I lost no time in getting out of the office, and was grateful indeed for the privilege.

At eleven the next night I brought $100,000 in banknotes and put them into the chief's hands, and shortly afterward he took his leave, with the brave old undimmed confidence in his eyes. An almost intolerable hour dragged to a close: then I heard his welcome tread, and rose gasping and tottered to meet him. How his fine eyes flamed with triumph! He said:

'We're compromised! The jokers will sing a different tune tomorrow! Follow me!'

He took a lighted candle and strode down into the vast vaulted basement where sixty detectives always slept, and where a score were now playing cards to while the time. I followed close after him. He walked swiftly down to the dim remote end of the place, and just as I succumbed to the pangs of suffocation and was swooning away he stumbled and fell over the outlying members of a mighty object, and I heard him exclaim as he went down:

'Our noble profession is vindicated. Here is your elephant!'

I was carried to the office above and restored with carbolic acid. The whole detective force swarmed in, and such another season of triumphant rejoicing ensued as I had never witnessed before. The reporters were called, baskets of champagne were opened, toasts were drunk, the hand-shaking and congratulations were continuous and enthusiastic. Naturally the chief was the hero of the hour, and his

happiness was so complete and had been so patiently and worthily and bravely won that it made me happy to see it, though I stood there a homeless beggar, my priceless charge dead, and my position in my country's service lost to me through what would always seem my fatally careless execution of a great trust. Many an eloquent eye testified its deep admiration for the chief, and many a detective's voice murmured, 'Look at him—just the king of the profession—only give him a clue, it's all he wants, and there ain't anything hid that he can't find.' The dividing of the $50,000 made great pleasure; when it was finished the chief made a little speech while he put his share in his pocket, in which he said, 'Enjoy it, boys, for you've earned it; and more than that—you've earned for the detective profession undying fame.'

A telegram arrived, which read:

'Monroe, Mich.: 10 p.m.

'First time I've struck a telegraph office in over three weeks. Have followed those footprints, horseback, through the woods, a thousand miles to here, and they get stronger and bigger and fresher every day. Don't worry—inside of another week I'll have the elephant. This is dead sure.

Darley, *Detective*'

The chief ordered three cheers for 'Darley, one of the finest minds on the force,' and then commanded that he be telegraphed to come home and receive his share of the reward.

So ended that marvelous episode of the stolen elephant.

The newspapers were pleasant with praises once more, the next day, with one contemptible exception. This sheet said, 'Great is the detective! He may be a little slow in finding a little thing like a mislaid elephant—he may hunt him all day and sleep with his rotting carcase all night for three weeks, but he will find him at last—if he can get the man who mislaid him to show him the place!'

Poor Hassan was lost to me for ever. The cannon-shots had wounded him fatally. He had crept to that unfriendly place in the fog; and there, surrounded by his enemies and in constant danger of detection, he had wasted away with hunger and suffering till death gave him peace.

The compromise cost me $100,000; my detective expenses were $42,000 more; I never applied for a place again under my Government; I am a ruined man and a wanderer in the earth—but my admiration for that man, whom I believe to be the greatest detective the world has ever produced, remains undimmed to this day, and will so remain unto the end.